This book belongs to:

_____

_____

First published 2017 by Parragon Books, Ltd.

Copyright © 2022 Cottage Door Press, LLC
5005 Newport Drive
Rolling Meadows, Illinois 60008

ISBN 978-1-64638-495-2

www.cottagedoorpress.com

Parragon is an imprint of Cottage Door Press, LLC.
Parragon® and the Parragon® logo are registered trademarks
of Cottage Door Press, LLC.

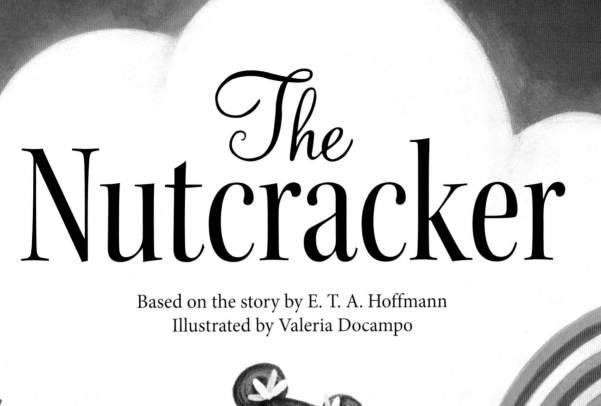

The Nutcracker

Based on the story by E. T. A. Hoffmann
Illustrated by Valeria Docampo

PaRRagon.

It was Christmas Eve and the snow was gently falling. Clara and her brother Fritz were very excited. That night, there would be a magnificent party with music and dancing, as well as lots of fantastic presents!

Fritz was busy with his toy soldiers, lining them up and giving them their orders.

Clara put the finishing touches on their
enormous tree. She hung shining ornaments and
candy canes tied with bows from the branches.
   "This is my favorite part," Clara said
to her brother as she lifted up a beautiful
fairy with delicate wings and a
sugarplum-colored dress.

At last, it was time for
the party to begin.

"The guests are arriving!"
cried Clara, peeping out of her
bedroom window.

Fritz came running over to see
who was crunching through the snow.

"Can you see Godfather
Drosselmeyer?" asked Clara.

"Yes, there he is waving!"
cried Fritz. "Come on!"

Their godfather was a famous
toymaker. He made the most magical
toys in the whole city. Clara and Fritz
could hardly wait to see what he had
brought for them.

Godfather Drosselmeyer hugged the children at the door, and with a flourish, he produced two gifts.

Fritz eagerly unwrapped a box of toy soldiers. For Clara, there was a wooden nutcracker in the shape of a soldier.

"Take good care of him," said Godfather Drosselmeyer. "He is very special."

"I love him," Clara whispered.

"Thank you."

"But he's a soldier," said Fritz. "He should be mine."

"You can't have him!" cried Clara.

Fritz tried to snatch the Nutcracker away
from her. He pulled and Clara tugged, and then …

CRACK!

The Nutcracker's leg snapped off!

Clara cradled the Nutcracker in her arms and wept.

"Don't cry, Clara," said her godfather gently. "This soldier has been wounded, but I can soon fix him."

Godfather Drosselmeyer pulled a little tool pouch from his pocket and quickly mended the Nutcracker, so that he looked as good as new.

"Oh, thank you," said Clara, drying her eyes. "I'll never let anyone hurt him again."

Everyone was dancing now and the house was
filled with music and laughter. Clara placed the
Nutcracker carefully under the Christmas tree
and went to join the party.

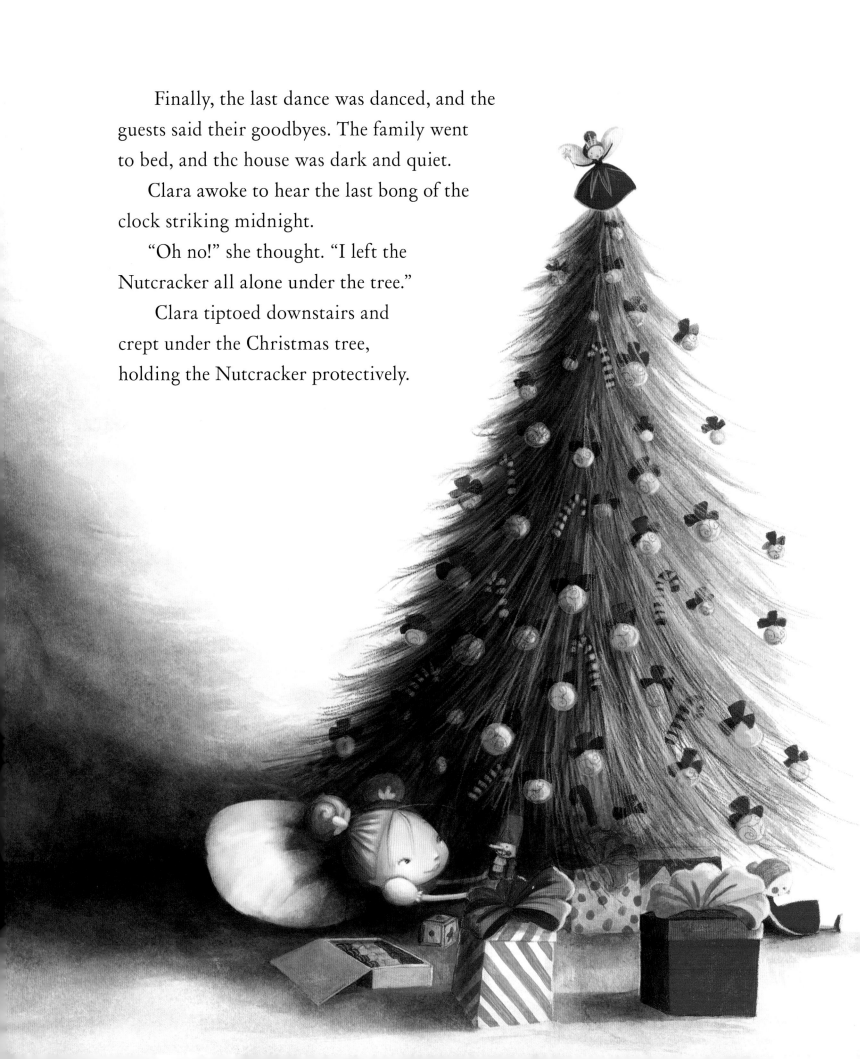

Finally, the last dance was danced, and the
guests said their goodbyes. The family went
to bed, and thc house was dark and quiet.

Clara awoke to hear the last bong of the
clock striking midnight.

"Oh no!" she thought. "I left the
Nutcracker all alone under the tree."

Clara tiptoed downstairs and
crept under the Christmas tree,
holding the Nutcracker protectively.

Suddenly, the tree started to grow
taller and taller! Or was it
just that Clara was shrinking?
   "What's happening?" she cried.

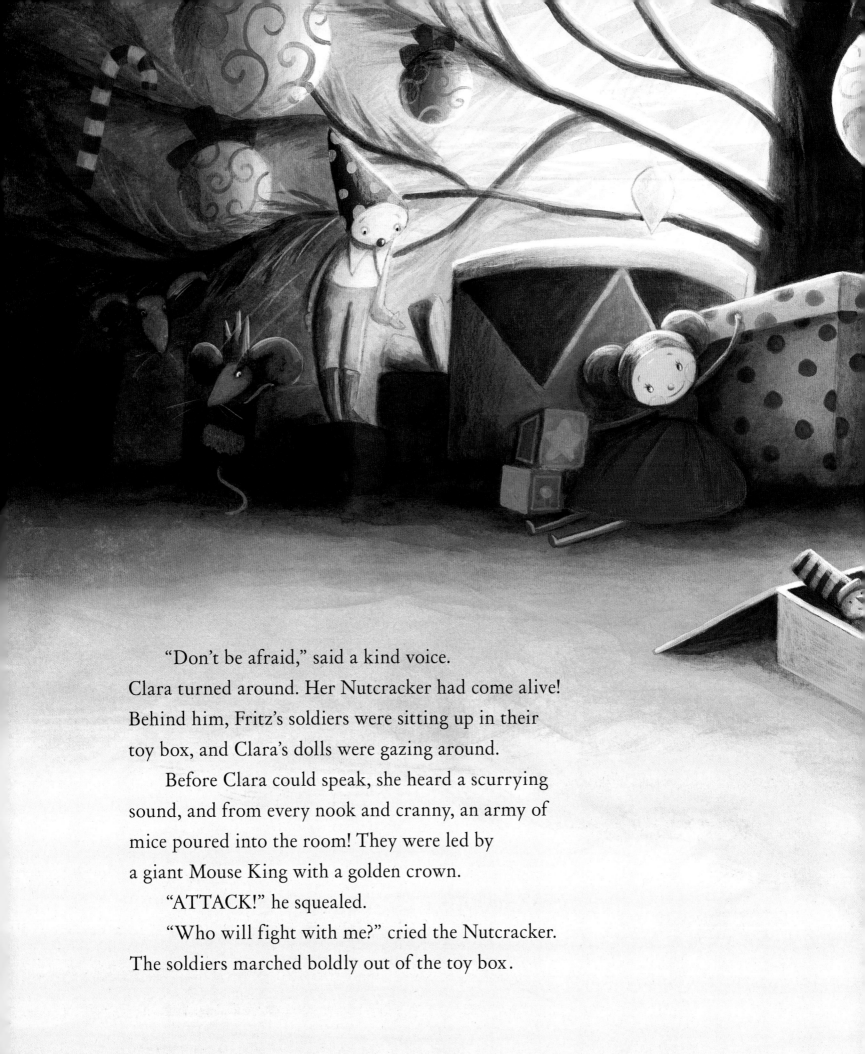

"Don't be afraid," said a kind voice.

Clara turned around. Her Nutcracker had come alive!
Behind him, Fritz's soldiers were sitting up in their
toy box, and Clara's dolls were gazing around.

Before Clara could speak, she heard a scurrying
sound, and from every nook and cranny, an army of
mice poured into the room! They were led by
a giant Mouse King with a golden crown.

"ATTACK!" he squealed.

"Who will fight with me?" cried the Nutcracker.
The soldiers marched boldly out of the toy box.

"TO BATTLE!" ordered the Nutcracker.
The soldiers shouted and cheered, and the
mice squealed and squeaked.

Suddenly, Clara saw the Mouse King spring toward her beloved Nutcracker, baring his teeth.

"No!' cried Clara. She snatched off her slipper and hurled it at the Mouse King. He fell to the ground with a cry, and his crown tumbled from his head.

With their leader defeated, the mice scurried away in fear. The battle was won!

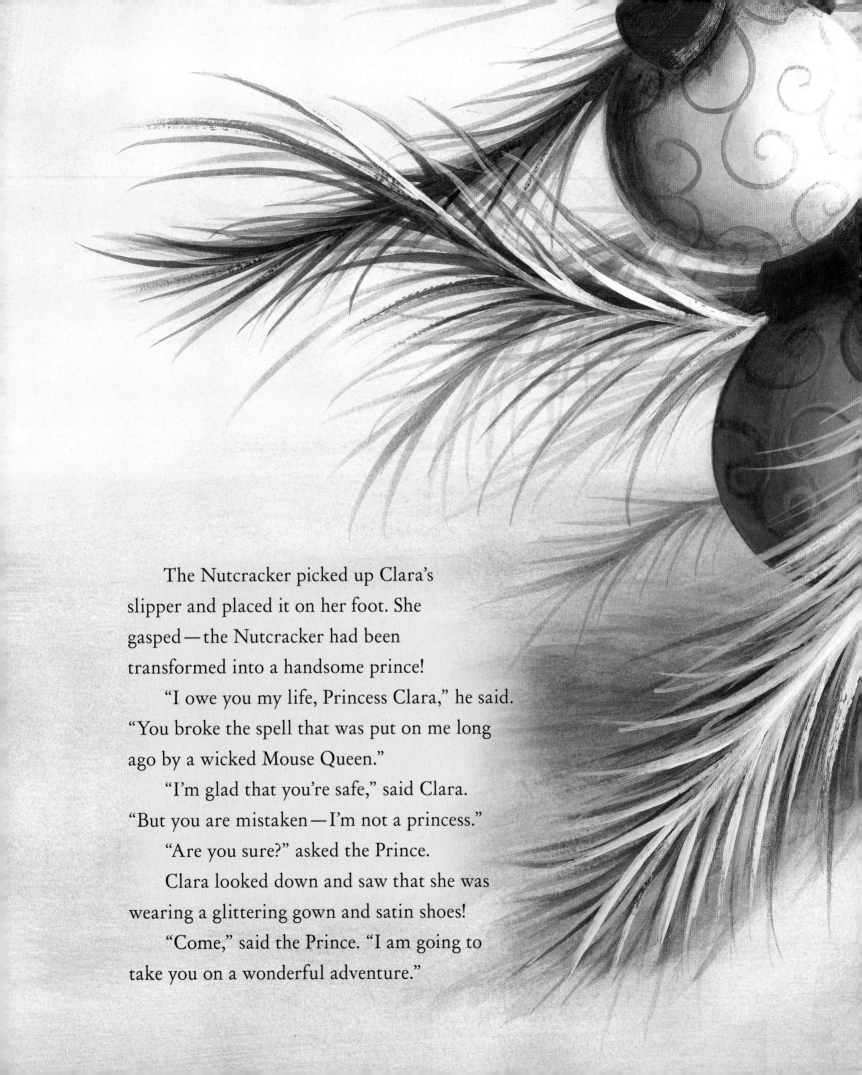

The Nutcracker picked up Clara's
slipper and placed it on her foot. She
gasped—the Nutcracker had been
transformed into a handsome prince!

"I owe you my life, Princess Clara," he said.
"You broke the spell that was put on me long
ago by a wicked Mouse Queen."

"I'm glad that you're safe," said Clara.
"But you are mistaken—I'm not a princess."

"Are you sure?" asked the Prince.

Clara looked down and saw that she was
wearing a glittering gown and satin shoes!

"Come," said the Prince. "I am going to
take you on a wonderful adventure."

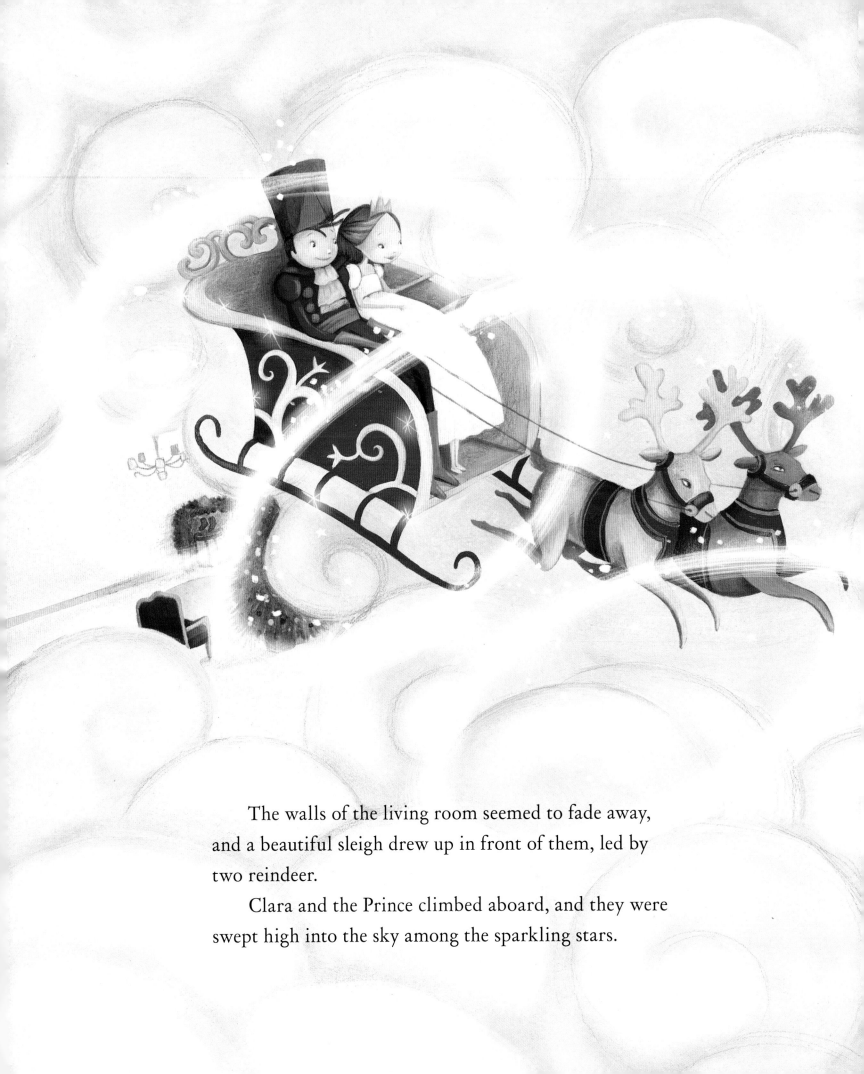

The walls of the living room seemed to fade away, and a beautiful sleigh drew up in front of them, led by two reindeer.

Clara and the Prince climbed aboard, and they were swept high into the sky among the sparkling stars.

Suddenly, Clara caught sight of a magical land down below. Lollipop trees shimmered on cotton-candy hills. There were gingerbread houses, rivers of honey, and an orange-scented breeze.

"Where are we?" gasped Clara.

"This is the Kingdom of Sweets," said the Prince.

The sleigh landed beside a rose-colored lake and changed into
a sea chariot pulled by dolphins. Swans swam beside them, and
shimmering fish leapt out of the water.

On the far side of the lake was a magnificent marzipan palace.
A fairy with delicate wings was waving to them from the gate.
"Look," said the Prince. "It's the Sugarplum Fairy!"

"Prince Nutcracker!" cried the fairy. "You are home at last."
"This is Princess Clara," said the Prince, as they stepped ashore.
"She saved my life and broke the Mouse Queen's spell."
The Sugarplum Fairy hugged Clara.
"Come and join the celebrations!" she said.

Inside the palace, Clara and the Prince feasted on delicious cakes and sweets.

They watched in wonder as dancers from every corner of the world whirled around the room.

Then it was the Sugarplum Fairy's turn. Clara had never seen such dancing! She twirled and twirled until all Clara could see was the blur of her plum-colored dress.

Clara's eyelids began to droop. Her adventures had made her tired. The sound of the music became fainter and fainter ...

When Clara woke on Christmas morning,
she found herself curled up under the Christmas tree
next to the Nutcracker. Toys were strewn across the
floor, and her parents were standing over her.

"What have you been doing?"
asked her father.

"Oh, I've had the most wonderful
adventure," said Clara.

She told her parents all about the
Mouse King, the Nutcracker Prince,
and the Kingdom of Sweets.

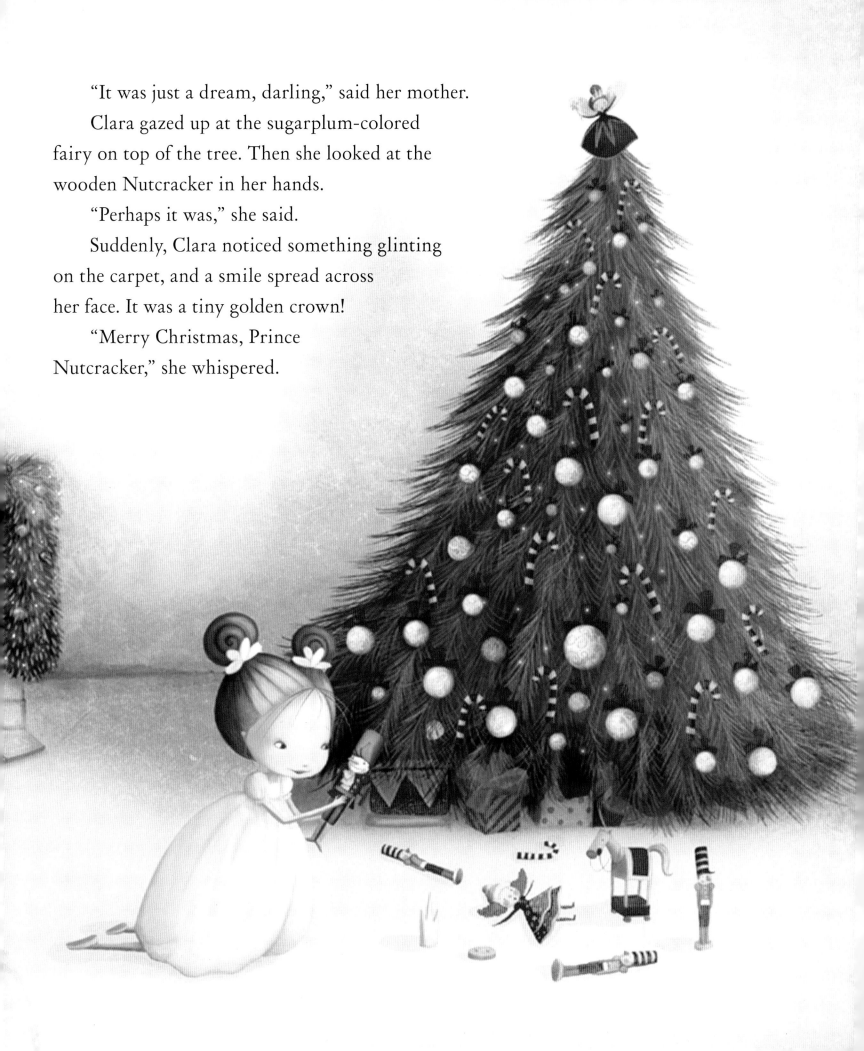

"It was just a dream, darling," said her mother.

Clara gazed up at the sugarplum-colored fairy on top of the tree. Then she looked at the wooden Nutcracker in her hands.

"Perhaps it was," she said.

Suddenly, Clara noticed something glinting on the carpet, and a smile spread across her face. It was a tiny golden crown!

"Merry Christmas, Prince Nutcracker," she whispered.